This Little Tiger
book belongs to:

_____

_____

_____

D0317909

3 8002 02178 727 2

For Poppy Rose, with love
~ M C B

For Kais Bahrani
~ T M

LITTLE TIGER PRESS
1 The Coda Centre,
189 Munster Road, London SW6 6AW
www.littletiger.co.uk
First published in Great Britain 2013
This edition published 2014
Text copyright © M Christina Butler 2013
Illustrations copyright © Tina Macnaughton 2013

M Christina Butler and Tina Macnaughton have asserted
their rights to be identified as the author and illustrator of this
work under the Copyright, Designs and Patents Act, 1988

One Special Christmas

M Christina Butler

Illustrated by Tina Macnaughton

LITTLE TIGER PRESS
London

It was Christmas Eve, and Little Hedgehog
was busy in his kitchen.

   "*We wish you a merry Christmas!*" he sang,
stirring his yummy cake mixture.

   Just then, something landed BUMP!
outside his window . . .

It was a sledge full of presents, with a note:
Dear Little Hedgehog, I have a terrible cold and need your help! Would you be able to deliver these Christmas presents for me? Thank you! Love, Santa.

"Oh my!" squeaked Little Hedgehog,
rushing to wrap up warm. "Don't
worry, Santa! I'm on my way!"

A big moon was shining in the dark sky as Little Hedgehog hurried up the hill to Mouse's house.

He squeezed
inside and tucked
three tiny presents under
the Christmas tree.
"Mouse and her babies
will be so excited!" he whispered.
"But I'd better be quick – there's
lots more to deliver!"

With a mighty push,
Little Hedgehog jumped
onto the sledge and zoomed
off, faster and faster
down the hill.

"Yippee!" he laughed.
"I'm just like Santa!"

"What was that?" cried Rabbit,
as the sledge sped past.

"It's Little Hedgehog!"
yelled Fox. "He's going
far too fast!"

Suddenly the sledge hit a snowdrift with a BUMP! and flew up into the air . . .

...CRASH!

"Little Hedgehog!" cried Rabbit and Fox, racing up and pulling him out of the snow.

"Thank you!" puffed Little Hedgehog. "But look – the presents are scattered everywhere! I have to deliver them for Santa!"

"We'll help," said Fox. "Great!" replied Little Hedgehog. "We can use my hat as a sack!"

So they tugged and heaved,
and they squashed
and squeezed . . .

until every last
present was in!

Laughing and giggling they sped
off again.

"Santa's helpers are coming!"
cried Little Hedgehog.

But as they passed a holly bush,
the hat caught on the prickly leaves
and the wool started to unravel . . .

The hat got
smaller and smaller . . .
and one by one, the
presents fell out!

"Oh no!" groaned Fox when at last they stopped the sledge. "The presents have gone!" "And look at my hat!" said Little Hedgehog. "What are we going to do?"

But just then, Badger
came wobbling down
the hill towards them.
"I followed the red wool,"
he chuckled. "I knew it
was from your hat,
Little Hedgehog!"

"You've found
Santa's presents!
Oh thank you, Badger!"
said Little Hedgehog.
"But I'll never deliver them
in time for Christmas now!"
"I'm sure you will,"
smiled Badger, "if we
all help!"

The friends dashed
through the
snow . . .

delivering
presents to
homes near
and far . . .

and high
and low . . .

working busily
through the
night.

The sky was turning pale blue and gold
by the time they had finished.

"Hooray!" cheered Little Hedgehog. "We did it!
Thank you, everyone. Santa will be so pleased!"

"What an adventure
I've had!" sighed
Little Hedgehog as
he walked home.
"I will miss my
lovely red hat
though!"

But as he opened
his door, he found
a surprise . . .

It was a present with a note:

For my wonderful Christmas helper.
Thank you! Love, Santa.

Inside was a brand new bobble hat –
hedgehog size!

"It's perfect!" cried Little Hedgehog.
"Thank you, Santa! What a special
Christmas this has been!"

For my wonderful
Christmas helper.
Thank you!
Love, Santa.

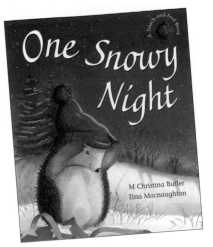

One Snowy Night

M Christina Butler
Tina Macnaughton

One Winter's Day

M Christina Butler
Illustrated by
Tina Macnaughton

One Starry Night

M Christina Butler
Tina Macnaughton

One Rainy Day

M Christina Butler
Illustrated by
Tina Macnaughton

One Christmas Night

M Christina Butler
Tina Macnaughton

One Special Day

M Christina Butler   Tina Macnaughton

Perfect presents for Little Hedgehog fans!

Collect them all!

For information regarding any of the above titles
or for our catalogue, please contact us:
Little Tiger Press, 1 The Coda Centre,
189 Munster Road, London SW6 6AW
Tel: 020 7385 6333 • Fax: 020 7385 7333
E-mail: contact@littletiger.co.uk • www.littletiger.co.uk